W9-CMI-812

Parents and Caregivers,

Stone Arch Readers are designed to provide enjoyable reading experiences, as well as opportunities to develop vocabulary, literacy skills, and comprehension. Here are a few ways to support your beginning reader:

• Talk with your child about the ideas addressed in the story.

• Discuss each illustration, mentioning the characters, where they are, and what they are doing.

• Read with expression, pointing to each word. You may want to read the whole story through and then revisit parts of the story to ensure that the meanings of words or phrases are understood.

• Talk about why the character did what he or she did and what your child would do in that situation.

• Help your child connect with characters and events in the story.

Remember, reading with your child should be fun, not forced. Each moment spent reading with your child is a priceless investment in his or her literacy life.

Gail Saunders-Smith, Ph.D.

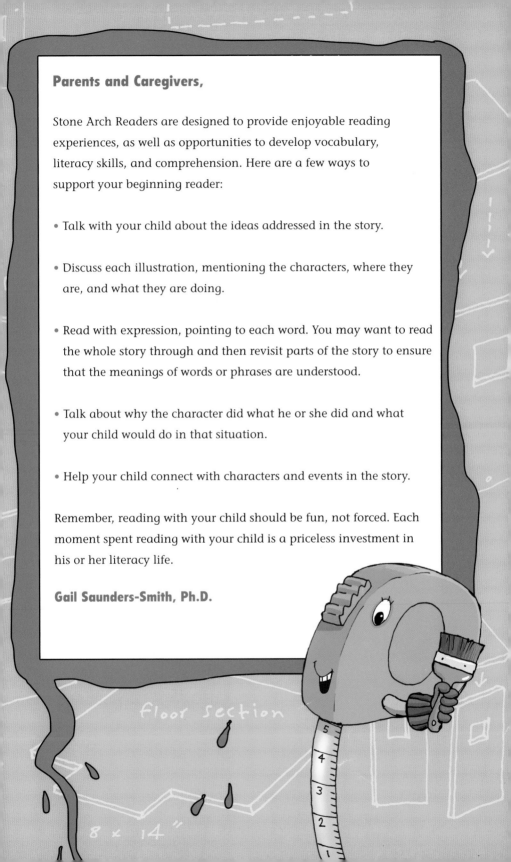

Stone Arch Readers

are published by Stone Arch Books
a Capstone Imprint
151 Good Counsel Drive, P.O. Box 669
Mankato, Minnesota 56002
www.capstonepub.com

Library of Congress Cataloging-in-Publication Data
Klein, Adria F. (Adria Fay), 1947-
  Tia Tape Measure / by Adria Klein ; illustrated by Andrew Rowland.
    p. cm. — (Stone Arch readers. Tool school)
  Summary: Tia Tape Measure helps measure shelves so the new library books
can be put away.
ISBN 978-1-4342-3046-1 (library binding)
ISBN 978-1-4342-3388-2 (pbk.)
  [1. Measurement—Fiction. 2. Tools—Fiction. 3. Libraries—Fiction. 4. Helpfulness—
Fiction.] I. Rowland, Andrew, 1962- ill. II. Title.
  PZ7.K678324Ti 2011
  [E]—dc22   2010050219

Reading Consultants:
Gail Saunders-Smith, Ph.D.
Melinda Melton Crow, M.Ed.
Laurie K. Holland, Media Specialist

Cover Concept: Russell Griesmer
Art Director/Designer: Kay Fraser
Production Specialist: Michelle Biedscheid

Printed in the United States of America in Melrose Park, Illinois.
032011
006112LKF11

Tia

NIAGARA FALLS PUBLIC LIBRARY

Tia Tape Measure

by Adria Klein

illustrated by Andy Rowland

Sammy Saw

Sophie Screwdriver

"Where is Tia?" asks Sophie.

"I don't know," says Sammy.

"We can't do this job without her," says Hank.

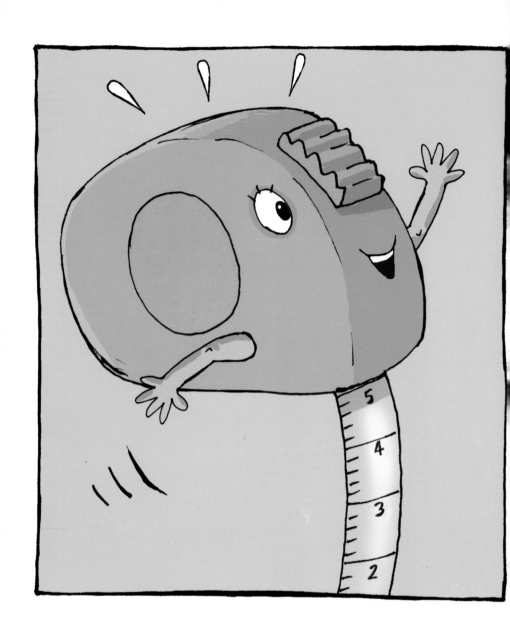

"Here I am!" says Tia. "What's going on?"

"The library got new shelves,"
says Hank.

"That's great!" says Tia.

"It is. But the library is a mess,"
says Hank.

"How can we help?" asks
Sammy.

"Follow me," says Hank.

Boxes and books were all over the library.

"This place is a mess,"
says Sophie.

"It sure is," says Hank.

"Where do we start?" asks Tia.

"First, let's put the books into piles," says Hank.

"Good idea," says Sammy.

"All the books are in piles.
Now what?" asks Tia.

"Now you need to get to work,"
says Hank.

"What should I do?" asks Tia.

"Measure everything!" says Sophie.

"No problem!" says Tia.

"Measure tall, measure small, measure twice, make it nice," says Tia.

"I need tall books for this shelf,"
she says.

"Here you go," says Hank.

"These fit great," says Tia.

"Measure tall, measure small,
measure twice, make it nice,"
says Tia.

"I need short books for this shelf," she says.

"Here you go," says Sophie.

"These fit great," says Tia.

"We're on a roll!" says Tia.

"We sure are," says Hank.

"The library is really looking good," says Sophie.

"Good work, Tia," says Sammy.

"Thank you," says Tia. "But
I couldn't do it without my
friends."

"Tools rule!" they shout.

STORY WORDS

library   boxes

shelves   measure

books   twice

Total Word Count: 230